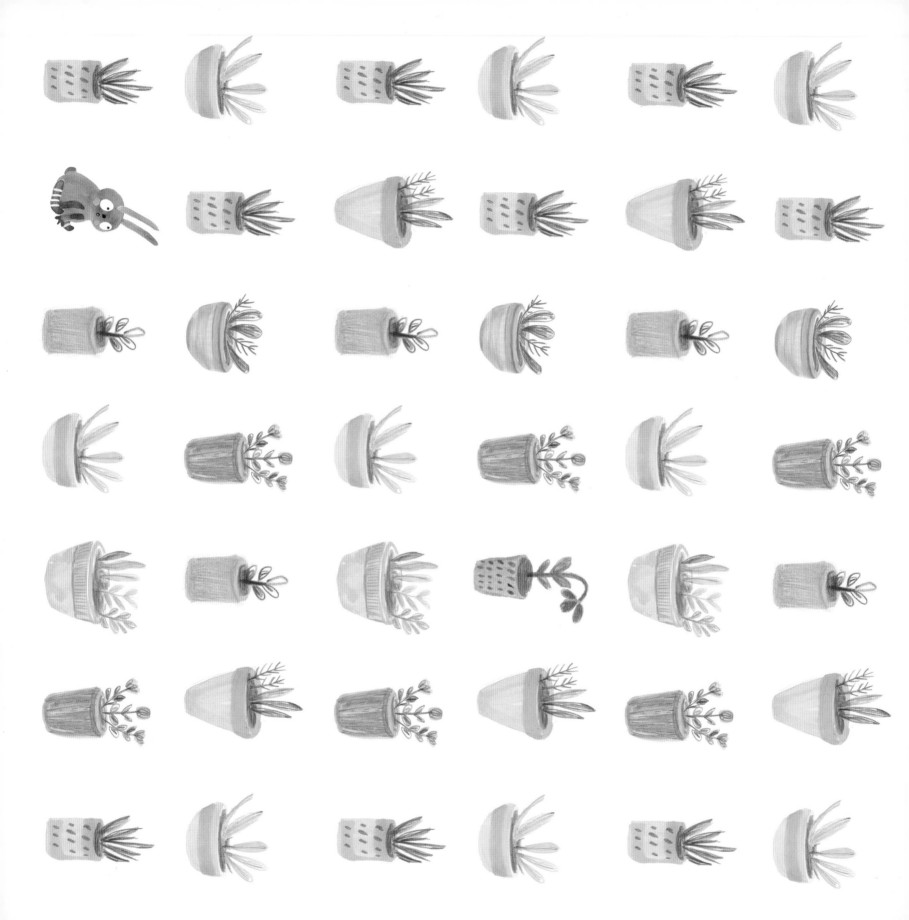

For Gina and Alex

First published in 2017 by Child's Play (International) Ltd
Ashworth Road, Bridgemead, Swindon SN5 7YD, UK

Published in USA by Child's Play Inc
250 Minot Avenue, Auburn, Maine 04210

Distributed in Australia by Child's Play Australia Pty Ltd
Unit 10/20 Narabang Way, Belrose, Sydney, NSW 2085

Text and illustrations copyright © 2017 Megan Brewis
The moral right of the author/illustrator has been asserted

ISBN 978-1-84643-999-5
CLP061216CPL0217995

Printed in Shenzhen, China

1 3 5 7 9 10 8 6 4 2

A catalogue record of this book
is available from the British Library

www.childs-play.com

HENRY and

BOO!

Megan Brewis

Henry didn't know where BOO had come from. He simply arrived one day.

Henry was having a nice cup of tea, and the next thing he knew, there was BOO, right next to the teapot!

Henry asked him to leave.

But BOO just said...

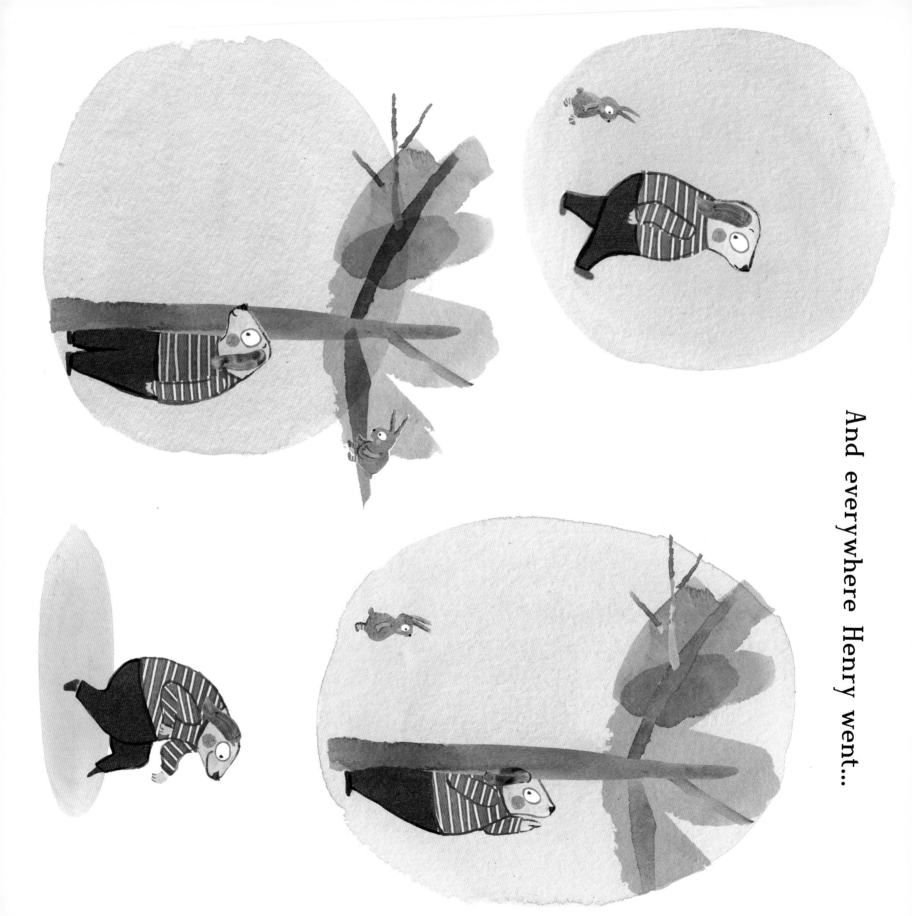

And everywhere Henry went...

And BOO said...

BOO went too.

And everything
Henry did...

BOO did too.

And BOO said...

BOO!!

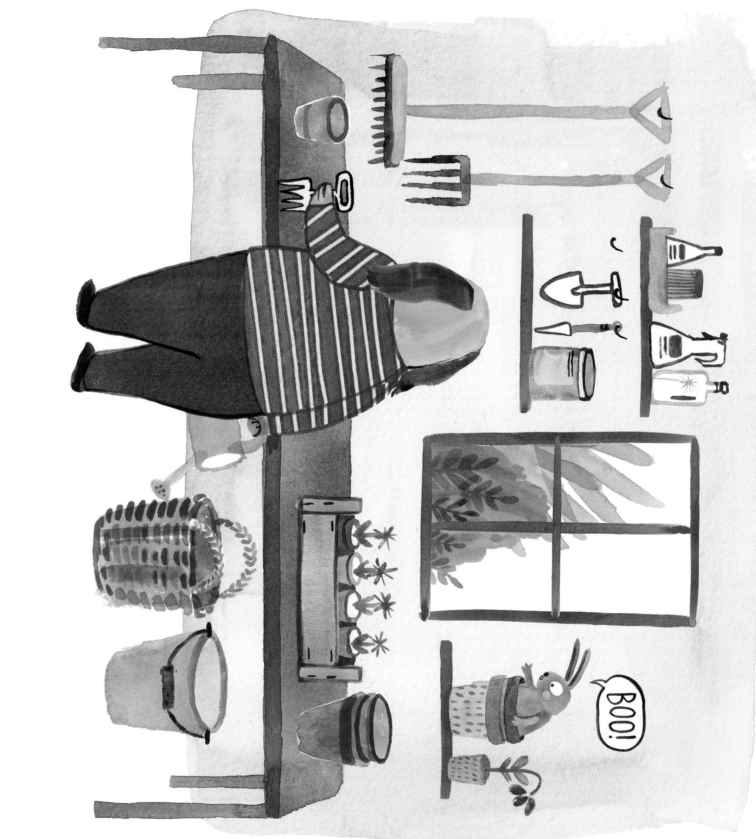

Henry tried to ignore BOO.

But BOO just said...

BOO?

So Henry tried to hide.

But BOO said, "BOO!"

In fact, BOO said "BOO!" a lot.
I mean, REALLY a lot.

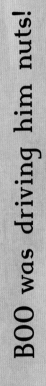

And quite frankly,
Henry had had enough.

BOO was driving him nuts!

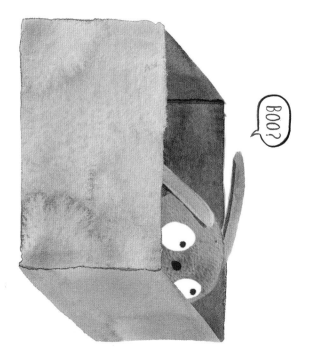

Just when Henry had thought
of a brilliant solution to his BOO problem...

"Aargh!
A bear!!"

And Henry felt quite faint...

It looked FIERCE!
And it seemed
HUNGRY!

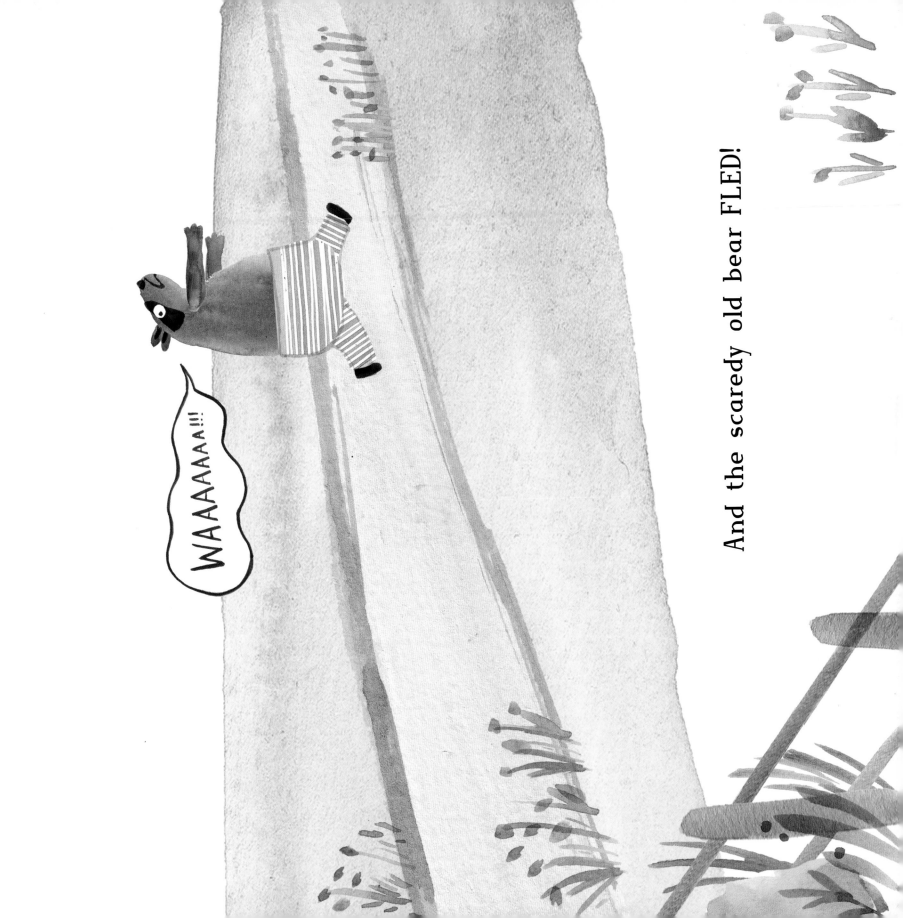

And the scaredy old bear FLED!

And BOO said...

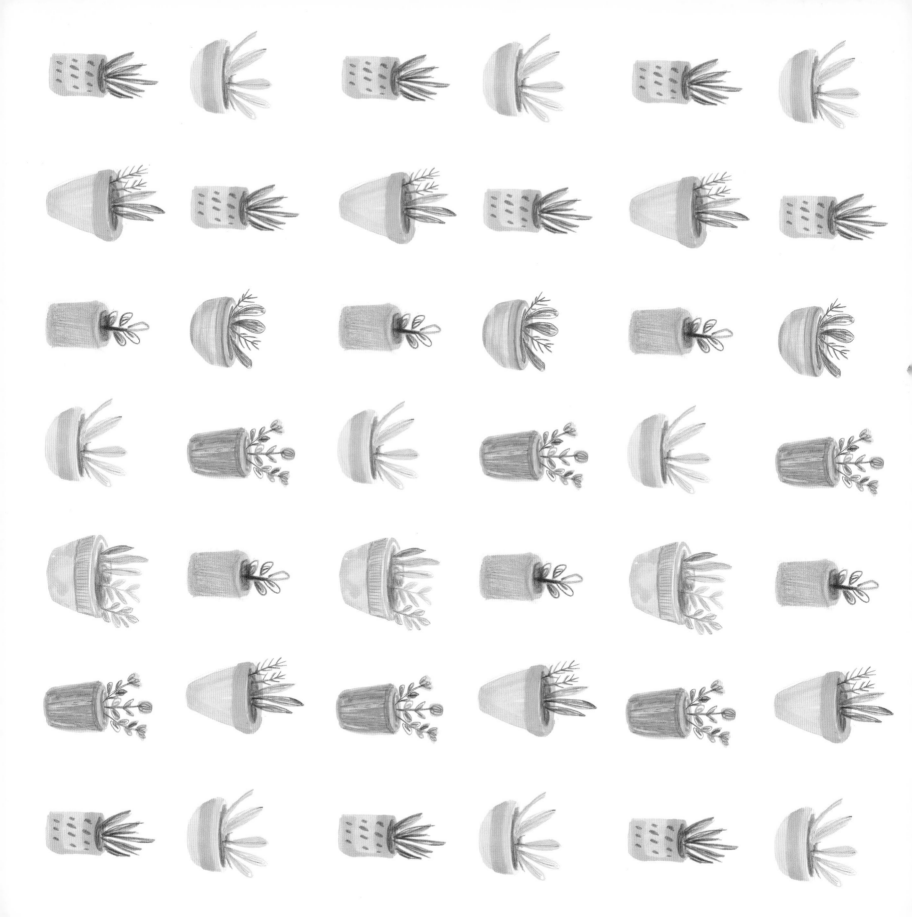